THE MOON FESTIVAL

A Chinese Mid-Autumn Celebration

Arlene Chan

Illustrations by
Nicolas Debon

UMBRELLA PRESS
Toronto

DEDICATION

Arlene Chan: To my family
Nicolas Debon: To Nathalie

PUBLISHER: Ken Pearson
DESIGN: John Lee, Heidy Lawrance Associates
CALLIGRAPHY: Ma Shiu-Yu
TRANSLATION OF THE POEM BY LI BAI: Baimei Sun

The People's Republic of China uses Pinyin, a romanization system of the Chinese language. It spells out the sound of Chinese characters into English words. Pinyin has been adopted by most Western newspapers and magazines and has been used for this book.

Canadian Cataloguing in Publication Data

Chan, Arlene
    The Moon festival: a Chinese mid-autumn celebration

Includes bibliographical references.

ISBN 1-895642-34-5

1. Folklore – China. 2. Children's stories, Chinese. 3. Mid-autumn Festival – Juvenile literature. I. Debon, Nicolas, 1968–   . II. Title.

GR335.4.M66C42 1998   j394.2'64'0951   C98-931908-3

Manufactured in Canada
A Three Panes and a Star Publication

UMBRELLA PRESS
56 Rivercourt Blvd.
Toronto, ON. M4J 3A4

Telephone: 416-696-6665
Fax: 416-696-9189
E-mail: umbpress@interlog.com
Website: www.interlog.com/~umbpress

THE MOON FESTIVAL

The most beautiful full moon rises in the evening sky on the fifteenth day of the eighth month in the Chinese calendar. This full moon is honored by people of Chinese origin throughout the world with the celebration known as the Moon Festival, or the Mid-Autumn Festival. On this night, the moon appears bigger, brighter and closer than at any other time of the year. For this one night only, the Chinese say, the moon is perfectly round and has special meaning.

The Moon Festival is one of the most popular Chinese celebrations of the year. It takes place in the middle of the three months that make up the autumn season in the Chinese calendar. For this reason, many people call it the Mid-Autumn Festival. In the Western calendar, this occurs around the month of September.

The Moon Festival almost certainly began as a harvest celebration to give thanks and to celebrate a bountiful crop.

The Chinese have a legend or story for nearly everything. Throughout centuries of time, Chinese storytellers have drawn on a wealth of tales about the moon. One of the most popular stories is the legend of the Moon Goddess, Chang O, considered one of the most beautiful woman in Chinese mythology. This legend, dating back to around 2000 BC, has been passed down through the generations by word of mouth. It is because of this that there are so many versions of the story, and the following is one of the most popular.

CHANG O AND THE MOON PALACE

Long ago, the world was very different than it is today. Ten bright suns, instead of one, circled the earth. These ten golden suns were the children of the Jade Emperor who ruled the heavens. Usually, they would come out individually and follow each other, in an orderly way, across the sky, but one day they came out all together, running wildly through the sky. The light from the combined suns was blinding, the heat unbearable. Animals collapsed. Rivers dried up. Forests burned. Even the rocks began to melt. The terrible effect of the blazing suns brought suffering and death to the people as famine became widespread.

The great Emperor Yao, a wise and compassionate man, was a ruler who cared for his people and put all his efforts into helping them. As the destruction caused by the ten suns increased by the day, the Emperor summoned Hou Yi, the most skilled archer in the kingdom. Hou Yi was ordered to return earth to its former beauty. "The false suns must be destroyed," said the Emperor, "or all life will come to an end." Hou Yi replied, "Emperor Yao, I will shoot them from the sky."

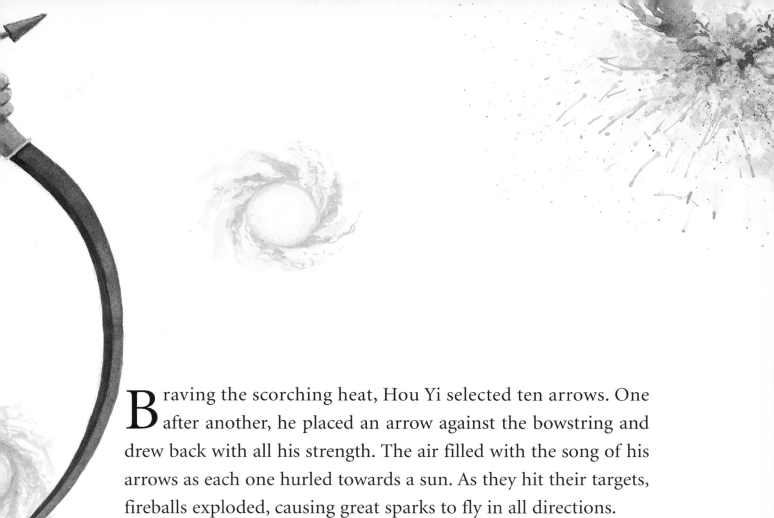

Braving the scorching heat, Hou Yi selected ten arrows. One after another, he placed an arrow against the bowstring and drew back with all his strength. The air filled with the song of his arrows as each one hurled towards a sun. As they hit their targets, fireballs exploded, causing great sparks to fly in all directions.

The wise Emperor knew that one sun had to remain to provide warmth and light for the earth. Creeping up behind Hou Yi, the Emperor quietly took one arrow. Hou Yi, too busy to notice, continued shooting down the suns.

Soon, there were no arrows left. He had shot down all but one of the suns. Exhausted from his task, Hou Yi looked into the blue sky at the one remaining sun. Suddenly, his ears filled with the shouts of the people. He had saved the world from destruction.

Word about Hou Yi's heroism spread far and wide. It reached across the mountains to the west where a powerful goddess lived. She was the Queen Mother of the West, a goddess with the head of a woman, the teeth of a tiger and an ugly body that ended in a leopard's tail. Living in her palace high above the clouds, she was the guardian of the elixir of life. She heard about Hou Yi's valiant deed and summoned him to her palace.

"I give you this magic potion as a reward for saving the world from destruction," she said. "Guard this precious powder well. It is made from a tree whose fruit gives everlasting life. When you take it, you will live forever." By giving him this magic potion, the Queen Mother of the West knew that Hou Yi would live forever and he would protect the world from disaster should too many suns re-appear.

Hou Yi returned home and hid his reward from his wife, Chang O. He wanted to wait for the best time to take this magical powder that would give him everlasting life.

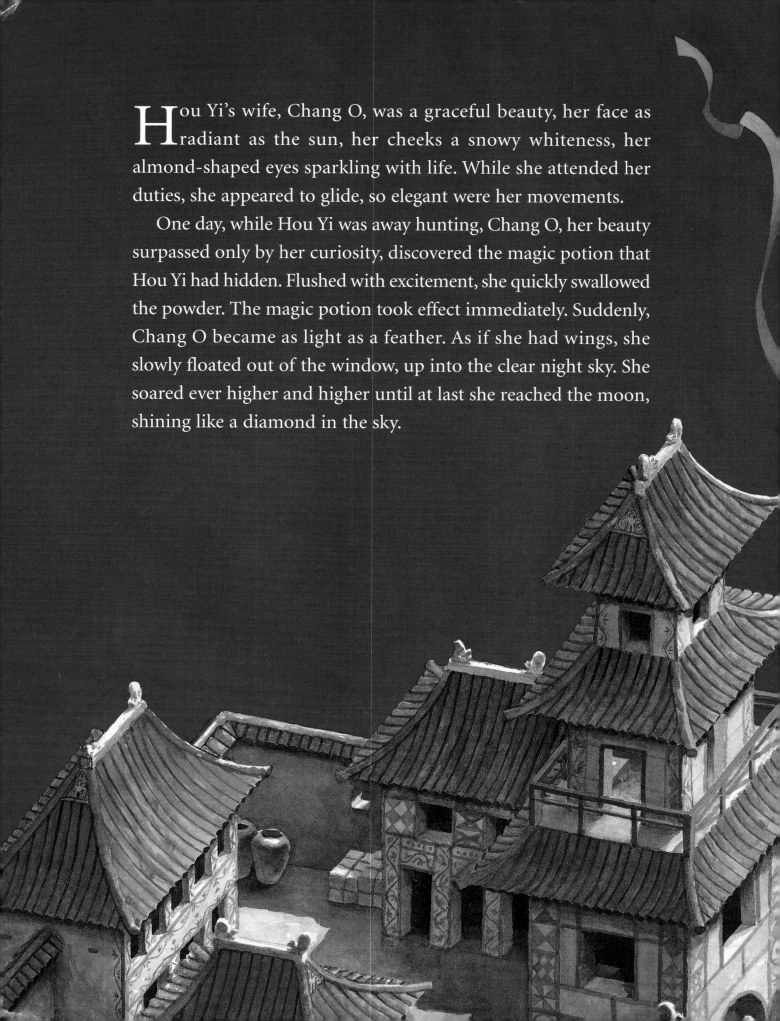

Hou Yi's wife, Chang O, was a graceful beauty, her face as radiant as the sun, her cheeks a snowy whiteness, her almond-shaped eyes sparkling with life. While she attended her duties, she appeared to glide, so elegant were her movements.

One day, while Hou Yi was away hunting, Chang O, her beauty surpassed only by her curiosity, discovered the magic potion that Hou Yi had hidden. Flushed with excitement, she quickly swallowed the powder. The magic potion took effect immediately. Suddenly, Chang O became as light as a feather. As if she had wings, she slowly floated out of the window, up into the clear night sky. She soared ever higher and higher until at last she reached the moon, shining like a diamond in the sky.

Upon reaching the moon, Chang O felt the intense cold. No living being could be seen. The only vegetation was cinnamon trees. Having taken the magic potion, she would now have to live forever on this lonely place. Her youth and beauty were to be hers forever, but sadly she was doomed to live alone on the moon.

When Hou Yi returned home from hunting, his wife was nowhere to be found. He searched for the magic potion but it too could not be found. He knew immediately what had happened. His wife had taken the magic potion and would now live without him on the moon for eternity.

Overcome with sorrow, he could do nothing to bring her back. Each night, Hou Yi peered into the sky searching for his beloved wife, Chang O, in hope of catching a glimpse of her on the moon.

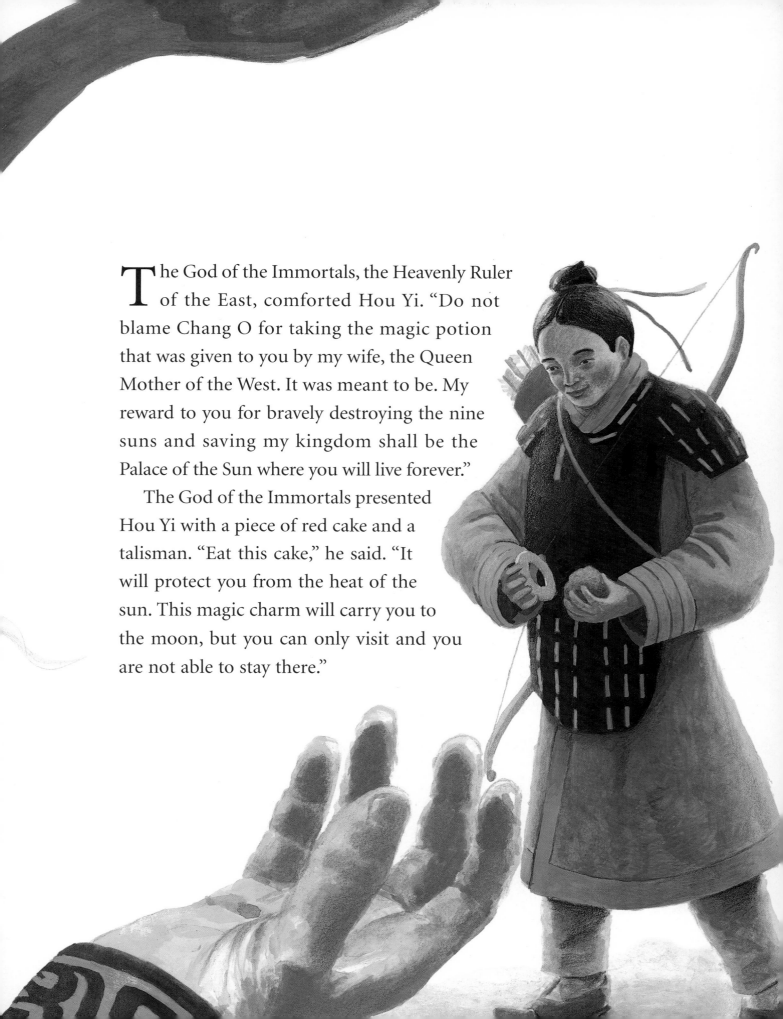

The God of the Immortals, the Heavenly Ruler of the East, comforted Hou Yi. "Do not blame Chang O for taking the magic potion that was given to you by my wife, the Queen Mother of the West. It was meant to be. My reward to you for bravely destroying the nine suns and saving my kingdom shall be the Palace of the Sun where you will live forever."

The God of the Immortals presented Hou Yi with a piece of red cake and a talisman. "Eat this cake," he said. "It will protect you from the heat of the sun. This magic charm will carry you to the moon, but you can only visit and you are not able to stay there."

Hou Yi ate the cake and fastened the talisman securely to his belt. Overjoyed with the thought of being reunited with his wife, he flew to the moon on a ray of sunlight. On the expanse of the cold moon, he saw Chang O, all alone. Seeing her husband, Chang O was filled with fear for having stolen his magic potion.

"Do not be afraid," he reassured her. "I am now living in the Palace of the Sun. I have been given the power to visit you here on the moon."

Magically, on the fifteenth day of every month, when the moon is fullest, the heavenly couple are happily united. That is why the full moon is so brilliant on that night. It is the joining of the sun and the moon that shines so brightly, and the brightest moon of the year occurs in mid-autumn.

Sadly, when the Bird of Dawn shakes the heavens with its shrill cry, Hou Yi must leave his beloved Chang O and return to the Palace of the Sun.

MORE MOON STORIES

I t is said that Chang O does not live alone on the moon and that many other immortals live there with her. The Three-Legged Toad, the Woodcutter, the Moon Hare, and the Old Man in the Moon commonly appear in the Moon Festival.

THE THREE-LEGGED TOAD

The three-legged toad is one of the immortals associated with the legend of the moon. Why this toad has only three legs is unknown. According to some versions of the story, the toad, with its grey ugly body and webbed feet, is, in fact, the beautiful Chang O. Her transformation to a toad was her punishment from the goddess, the Queen Mother of the West, for stealing the magic potion of immortality from her husband, Hou Yi.

THE WOODCUTTER

The woodcutter, Wu Gang, is said to live on the moon. If you look carefully, you can see him trying to chop down a cinnamon tree. Every time he makes a cut to this gigantic tree with his axe, the deep gash closes up. Without the luxury of sleep or rest, he has been trying to do this for countless centuries. How did this woodcutter come to end up with this frustrating and miserable life? Some say that this was his punishment for making the gods angry.

THE MOON HARE

The Moon Hare is one of the most favorite characters of the Moon Festival. The hare is the chief pharmacist, spending all his time making the drug of immortality. He is always working under a cinnamon tree whose leaves and bark provide valuable ingredients for his magic potion. If you look closely, you can see his profile in the dark spots on the moon.

The story of the hare on the moon can likely be traced to a Buddhist legend. According to the story, Buddha wanted to have some food and water for his followers. All the animals in the forest busied themselves and searched for the best that they could find for their beloved Buddha. Sadly, the hare could not find anything more than herbs and grasses. Ashamed about his lack of worthy offerings, he made the best sacrifice possible: himself. Seeing a cooking fire, the hare threw himself onto the flames. So moved was Buddha that he rewarded the hare for his supreme sacrifice by granting him an eternal place on the moon.

THE OLD MAN IN THE MOON

For the romantic at heart, there is the Old Man in the Moon. He is the universal matchmaker who arranges all marriages from his seat on the moon. He keeps a book with the names of the couples that he will match. On the special night of the Moon Festival, he can be found busily tying together couples with invisible red silk thread. Young women put great faith in him. They hope to have a vision of their future husbands on this night.

THE REVOLT AGAINST THE MONGOLS

A long time ago, a great army of mounted Mongol warriors thundered across China's northern border. There was no stopping the military force of these unequalled horsemen, the descendants of Genghis Khan. They conquered China, killing untold numbers of people.

The Mongols were cruel to the Chinese. They treated them as slaves. They stole from the storekeepers, roaming drunk through the streets. Many Chinese households were forced to have a Mongol soldier live among them. These conquering soldiers had to be obeyed, no matter how unreasonable their requests.

With the Moon Festival approaching, the Chinese planned a secret rebellion. They made thousands of moon cakes filled with tiny pieces of rolled paper containing messages to alert the Chinese people about the uprising. The plan to overthrow the Mongols spread quickly among the people.

On the day of the Moon Festival, there was much excitement. The Mongols thought the happy mood was because of the celebration of the Moon Festival. At midnight, huge fires broke out in the hills, signalling the attack, and the people then poured into the streets.

Soon, the fierce Chinese fighters defeated the Mongols. The new Chinese dynasty was called the Ming dynasty. The leader of the rebellion, a man with humble beginnings, became the first emperor of the Ming dynasty, one of the longest and most prosperous dynasties of Chinese history.

Since that triumphant overthrow of the Mongols, moon cakes have been a favorite delicacy. Today, you may find a square piece of paper, like the messages in the legend, attached to the bottom of the cake or pasted on top of the cake box. It is not unusual to see a dash of red coloring on moon cakes. This symbolizes the great victory over the Mongols.

THE EMPEROR DECREES THE CELEBRATION OF THE MOON

The origins of the Moon Festival are lost in the past. Some say that the celebration of the Moon Festival started during the Tang Dynasty (618-907) when one of the rulers, Emperor Xuan Zong (712-756), dreamed of visiting the moon. He saw the Moon Hare making the magic potion of immortality, and Chang O and hundreds of fairies, dressed in colorful feather robes, dancing beneath the cinnamon trees. Heavenly music filled the air. When the emperor awoke from his dream, he ordered a celebration of the moon.

Some say that the Emperor was so inspired by the heavenly music that he wrote down the melody from memory, thus beginning the Chinese passion for music and theater.

THE IMMORTALITY OF POETRY, LI BAI

The moon, with all its legendary characters, has inspired countless poets, writers, musicians and artists. Numerous stories, shadow puppet-plays and operas feature Chang O, the Moon Goddess. She represents our ongoing search for immortality, the magic potion that will preserve our youth and beauty forever.

Li Bai, one of the greatest poets of the Tang Dynasty, is called the Immortal of Poetry. One of his poems is so popular that almost every Chinese student knows it by heart. This poem reveals the deep place the moon holds in the hearts of the Chinese.

The bright moonlight in front of my bed

牀 前 明 月 光

Looks like white frost on top of the land.

疑 是 地 上 霜

Raising my head, I gaze at the moon.

舉 頭 望 明 月

Lowering my head, I think of my homeland.

低 頭 思 故 鄉

MOON CAKES

Moon cakes are the traditional food eaten during the festival. Even though these pastries come in different sizes, they are usually round to look like the full moon. Their roundness symbolizes the completeness and togetherness of the family. They are made of flour and sugar, filled with nuts, mashed red beans, lotus seeds, Chinese dates or other ingredients. Often, there is a cooked egg yolk in the center. When the moon cake is cut open, the yolk resembles the yellow moon.

Traditionally, moon cakes were baked to a golden brown like a small cake. Today, they are prepared in new and different ways. It is not unusual to find them made of fruit, ice cream, yogourt and jelly.

During the days of the emperors, the Imperial chefs made large moon cakes. They were carved with elaborate designs of the Moon Goddess, the Moon Hare, the Three-Legged Toad or groves of cinnamon trees. Today, these designs are often stamped on the pastries.

A month before the Moon Festival, Chinese bakeries, supermarkets and restaurants are brimming with a variety of moon cakes. According to an old Chinese saying, even to dream of a moon cake foretells riches.

CUSTOMS AND CELEBRATIONS

It is in the setting of different legends and beliefs that the Moon Festival is celebrated. In ancient China, the Moon Festival was a celebration for women. Because the moon was considered female, the women in each home organized the festivities.

The women put a poster on the wall. It showed the Moon Hare making the magic potion of immortality. Some put clay statues of the Moon Hare on an altar, a special table, in the courtyard under the light of the moon.

Apples, oranges, peaches, pomegranates, grapes and melons were stacked on plates for the altar. All these fruit, as round as the full moon, symbolized the completeness and togetherness of the family. The many seeds in the melons and pomegranates represented the number of children the family wanted to have. The apples and grapes symbolized fertility, the peaches long life and happiness. They represented the hopes of any Chinese family — many children and long life.

At midnight, families gathered together in front of the altar. They burned candles and incense, as well as the poster of the Moon Hare, as gifts to the moon. The women and the girls in the home bowed before the altar.

Today, these rites are not commonly observed. What has remained, however, is the tradition of family and friends getting together. Children go to parks, light small candles, munch on moon cakes and enjoy moon gazing. Young couples sit holding hands on the river banks and park benches looking at the moon.

Families and friends exchange pears, grapes, pomegranates and moon cakes as gifts. *Pomelos*, or Chinese grapefruit, are also popular gifts. The Chinese word for "pomelo" is *you*. This word sounds like the word meaning "protection" and expresses the hope that the moon will protect the family in the coming year.

Another Moon Festival treat is the bat nut. Children especially enjoy eating these nuts that look like scary flying bats. Once the hard shells are peeled, the centers, which taste like chestnut, can be enjoyed.

Lanterns enliven the festivities. They are made from colored paper or silk, stretched onto bamboo frames. Inside are small candles that light up the radiant colors and elaborate shapes. These cause some of them to float into the night sky, carrying away bad luck, as some believe. Many are hung from ceilings and balconies. Most are paraded through the streets under the moonlight. Trees, colorfully decorated with them, are known as Mid-Autumn Festival trees. In Singapore, the Moon Festival is called the Lantern Festival.

The lanterns symbolize Chinese beliefs. A lantern, shaped like a carp or goldfish, will bring good luck, especially in school. A butterfly lantern will bring you long life. Modern lanterns are often designed like airplanes, spaceships and cartoon heroes. One of the most common lantern shapes is that of the Moon Hare. The more lanterns, the better. The Chinese word for lantern sounds like the word for fertility. The more lanterns you have, the more children you will have.

In China, one of the most famous places to look at the full moon is at the West Lake in Hangzhou. Chinese emperors over centuries of time have celebrated the Festival on the shores of this celebrated lake. They built palaces with large doorways, circular in shape, and pools to reflect the moon's beauty.

In Hong Kong, dragon and lion dancers weave their way through the streets. Victoria Peak and other hilltops are popular places to enjoy the moon. Parks are ablaze with thousands of lanterns. They are starry fairylands as children and their families sit with their lanterns and candles awaiting the rising of the full moon.

People celebrate festivals in Taiwan as they have for hundreds of years. They have picnics and climb the hills to catch the best view of the full moon. Favorite places to watch the moon are often near lakes and pools where the moon's reflection enhances the magic of the celebration.

Every year, during the Moon Festival, Chinese communities around the world are enchanted by the moon. And, no matter how far away you are from your family and friends, its magical charm will bring your good wishes to them all.

嫦娥	Chang O	月老	Old Man in the Moon
后羿	Hou Yi	吳剛	Wu Gang
玉皇	Jade Emperor	李白	Li Bai
堯帝	Emperor Yao	中秋節	Mid-Autumn Festival
西王母	Queen Mother of the West	玄宗	Emperor Hsuan Tsung

FURTHER READING

Birch, Cyril. *Chinese myths and fantasies.* London: Oxford University Press, 1961.

Hoe, Ban Seng. *Beyond the golden mountain.* [Ottawa]: Canadian Museum of Civilization, 1989.

Law, Joan and Barbara E. Ward. *Chinese festivals.* Hong Kong: South China Morning Post, © 1982.

Russell, Ching Yeung. *Moon Festival.* Honesdale, Penn.: Boyd Mills Press, 1997.

Sanders, Tao Tao Liu. *Dragons, gods & spirits from Chinese mythology.* Vancouver: Douglas & McIntyre, 1980.

Stepanchuk, Carol and Charles Wong. *Mooncakes and hungry ghosts: festivals of China.* San Francisco: China Books and Periodicals, 1991.

Stepanchuk, Carol. *Red eggs & dragon boats.* Berkeley, CA: Pacific View Press, 1994.